Published by Doubleday, a division of
Bantam Doubleday Dell Publishing Group, Inc.,
666 Fifth Avenue, New York, New York 10103

Library of Congress Cataloging-in-Publication Data
Flack, Marjorie, 1897–1958.
[Angus and ducks]
Angus and the ducks / told and pictured by Marjorie Flack.
p.   cm.
Reprint. Originally published: Angus and ducks. Garden City, N.Y.
Doubleday, Doran, 1930.
Summary: A curious Scotch terrier decides to investigate the
strange noise coming from the other side of the hedge.
1. Dogs—Juvenile fiction.   [1. Dogs—Fiction. 2. Ducks—
Fiction.]   I. Title.
PZ10.3.F594A1   1989
[E]—dc19   88-3627
CIP
AC

ISBN 0-385-07213-9
ISBN 0-385-07600-2 (lib. bdg.)
ISBN 0-385-26669-3 (pbk.)

Angus
and the Ducks

TOLD AND PICTURED BY
MARJORIE FLACK

DOUBLEDAY

NEW YORK   LONDON   TORONTO   SYDNEY   AUCKLAND

Once there was a very young little dog whose name was Angus, because his mother and his father came from Scotland.

Although the rest of Angus was quite small, his head was very large and so were his feet.

Angus was curious about many places and many things:

He was curious about WHAT lived under the sofa and in dark corners and

WHO was the little dog in the mirror.

He was curious about Things-Which-Come-Apart and those Things-Which-Don't-Come-Apart; such as SLIPPERS and gentlemen's SUSPENDERS and things like that.

Angus was also curious about Things-Outdoors
but he could not find out much about them because
of a leash.

The leash was fastened at one end to the collar around his neck and at the other end to **SOMEBODY ELSE.**

But Angus was most curious of all
about a NOISE
which came
from
the OTHER SIDE of
the large green hedge
at the end of
the garden.

The noise usually sounded like this:
Quack!   Quack!   Quackety!
         Quack!!

But sometimes it sounded like this:
         Quackety!   Quackety!
                  Quackety!
                        Quack!!

One day the door between OUTDOORS and INDOORS was left open by mistake; and out went Angus without the leash or SOMEBODY ELSE.

Down the little path he ran until he
came to the large green hedge at the end
of the garden.

He tried to go around it but it was much
too long.   He tried to go over it but it was much
too high.   So Angus went under the large green hedge

and came

out on the OTHER SIDE.

There, directly in front of hi

...ere two white DUCKS.
...hey were marching forward,
...ne-foot-up and one-foot-
                    down.

...uack!   Quack!

          Quackety!

                Quack!!!

Angus said.

WOO-OO-OOF!!!

Away went the DUCKS all of a flutter.

Quackety!   Quackety!

Quackety!   Quackety!

Quackety!!!

Angus followed after.

Soon the DUCKS stopped by a stone watering trough under a mulberry tree.

Angus stopped, too.   Each DUCK dipped a yellow bill in the clear cool water.   Angus watched. Each DUCK took a long drink of the cool clear water.   Still Angus watched.   Each DUCK took another long drink of cool clear water.

Then Angus said:

WOO-OO-OOF!!!

Away the DUCKS scuttled and

Angus lapped the cool clea
water.

Birds sang in the m
berry tree.

The Sun made patte
through the leaves
over the gra

The DUCKS talked together:

Quack! Quack!

Quack!

Then:

HISS-S-S-S-S-S-S!!!

The first DUCK nipped Angus's tail!

HISS-S-S-S-S-S-S!!!

Angus scrambled under the large green hedge,

scurried up the little path,

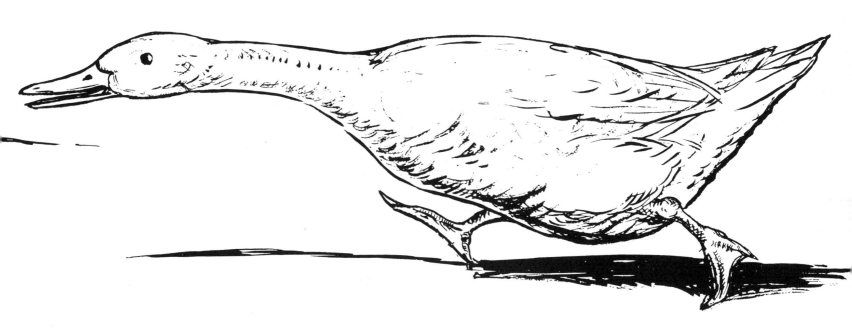

scampered into the house

and crawled under the sofa.

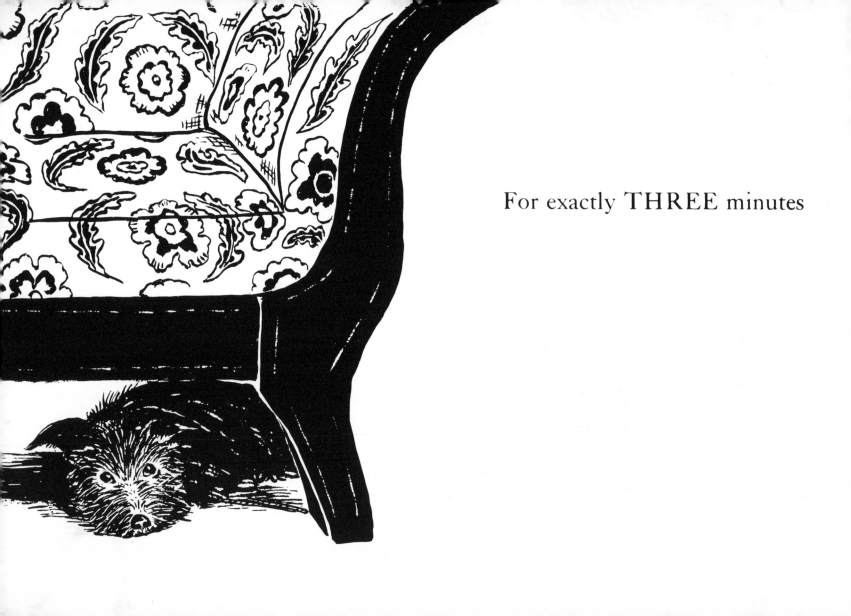

For exactly THREE minutes

by the clock, Angus was

NOT curious about
anything
at
all.